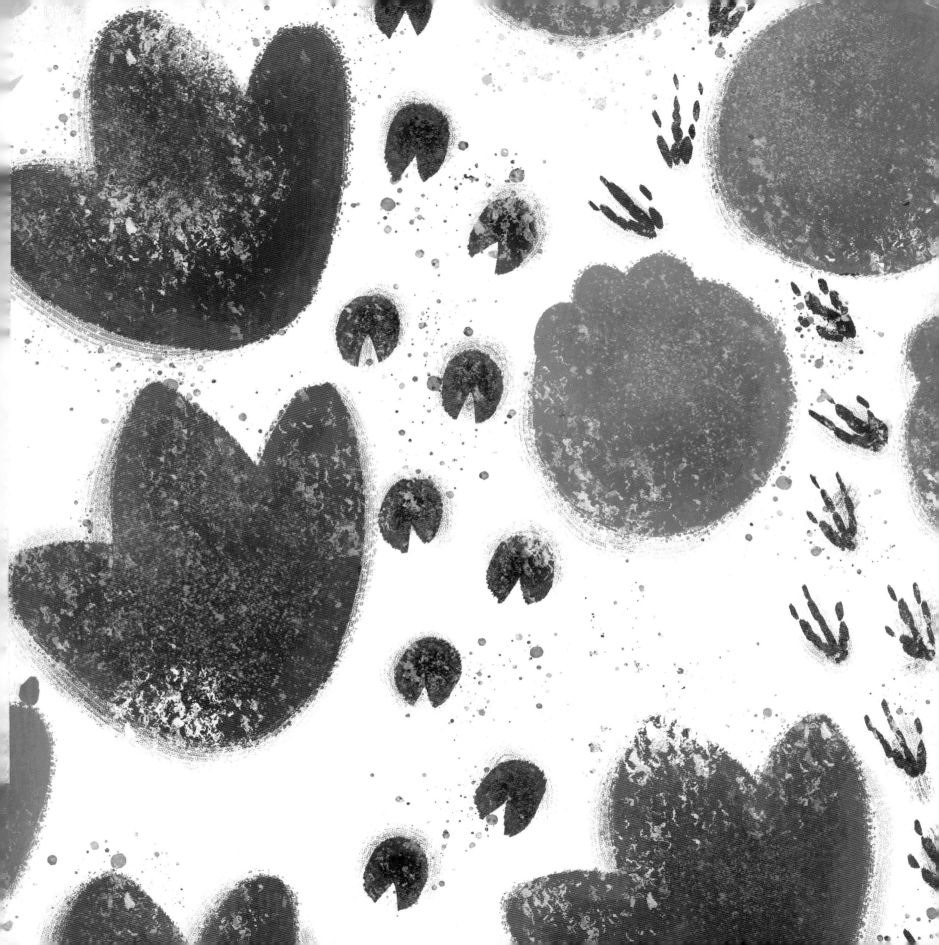

tiger tales

5 River Road, Suite 128, Wilton, CT 06897
Published in the United States 2017
Originally published in Great Britain 2017
by Little Tiger Press
Text by Becky Davies
Text copyright © 2017 Little Tiger Press
Illustrations copyright © 2017 Ben Whitehouse
ISBN-13: 978-1-68010-063-1
ISBN-10: 1-68010-063-7
Printed in China
LTP/1800/1836/0317
For more insight and activities, visit us at www.tigertalesbooks.com

Old MacDino Had a Farm

by Becky Davies

Illustrated by Ben Whitehouse

tiger tales

Old MacDino had a farm, E-I-E-I-O!

And on this farm he had a...

Diplodocus!
(dih-PLOD-uh-kus)

E-I-E-I-O!

With a **Munch! Munch!** here,
and a **Munch! Munch!** there,

Here a **Munch!** there a **Munch!**,
everywhere a **Munch! Munch!**

Old MacDino had a farm,
E-I-E-I- **Argh!**

Old MacDino had a farm, E-I-E-I-O!
And on this farm he had a...

Pterodactyl!!
(TARE-uh-DACK-tul)

E-I-E-I-O!

With a **Swoosh! Swoosh!** here,
and a **Swoosh! Swoosh!** there,

Here a **Swoosh!** there a **Swoosh!**,
everywhere a **Swoosh! Swoosh!**

Old MacDino had a farm,

E-I-E-I- **Oops!**

Old MacDino had a farm, E-I-E-I-O!
And on this farm he had a... **Stegosaurus!**
E-I-E-I-O!
(STEG-uh-SAWR-us)

With a **Stomp! Stomp!** here,
and a **Stomp! Stomp!** there,

Here a **Stomp!** there a **Stomp!**,
everywhere a **Stomp! Stomp!**

Old MacDino had a farm,
E-I-E-I- **Boing!**

Old MacDino had a farm,

E-I-E-I-O!

And on this farm he had a...

Triceratops!

(try-SAIR-uh-tops)

E-I-E-I-O!

With a **Crash! Smash!** here,
and a **Crash! Smash!** there,

Here a **Crash!** there a **Smash!**,
everywhere a **Crash! Smash!**

Old MacDino had a farm,

E-I-E-I- Whoa!

Yikes!

Old MacDino had a farm, E-I-E-I-O!

Old MacDino had a farm, E-I-E-I-O!
And on this farm he had a...

Tyrannosaurus rex!

(tye-RAN-uh-SAWR-us reks)

E-I-E-I-O!

With a **Roar! Roar!** here,
and a **Roar! Roar!** there,

Here a **Roar!** there a **Roar!**,
everywhere a **Roar! Roar!**

Old MacDino had a farm,

E-I-E-I- RUN!

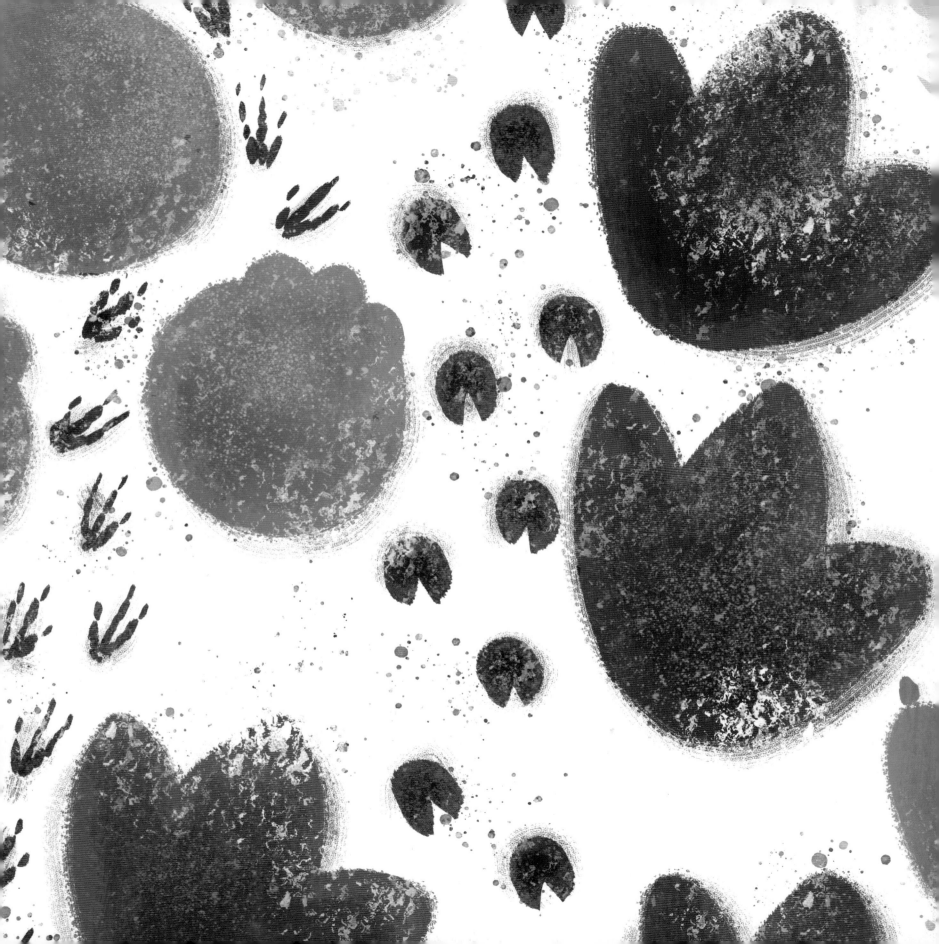